FRANK AND BEAN

FOOD TRUCK FIASCO

FRANK AND BEAN

FOOD TRUCK FIASCO

JAMIE MICHALAK

illustrated by BOB KOLAR

CANDLEWICK PRESS

For my dad,
a cool bean

JM

For Chef Gareth

BK

First edition 2022

Library of Congress Catalog Card Number pending
ISBN 978-1-5362-1441-3

22 23 24 25 26 27 CCP 10 9 8 7 6 5 4 3 2 1

Printed in Shenzhen, Guangdong, China

This book was typeset in New Century Schoolbook.
The illustrations were created digitally.

Candlewick Press
99 Dover Street
Somerville, Massachusetts 02144

www.candlewick.com

CONTENTS

F
ART
OF
CHILL

Chapter 1

FUN ON WHEELS

This is Frank.

This is Frank's tea.

This is Frank's book.

This is Frank's yoga mat.

Everything here is Frank's.

"Ahh!" he says. "Peace and quiet at last!"

But then he hears . . .

HONK!

HONK!

HONK!

This is Bean.

This is Bean's new hat.

This is Bean's new apron.

This is Bean's new food truck.

Everything here is Bean's.

"HI, FRANK!" shouts Bean. "IT IS I, BEAN!"

“What is THAT?” Frank asks.

“This is fun on wheels,” says Bean. “This is a rolling party. This is . . . a food truck!”

“Where are you going in it?” Frank asks.

“I am going to Food Truck Friday,” says Bean. “The one who makes the best food wins a prize! Care for a donut?”

“Yes,” says Frank.

“What topping would you like?” Bean asks.

“Pickles,” says Frank.

Bean makes an ick face.

“No pickles,” he says. “Would you like this donut instead? I call it Big Bean Candy Mountain.”

“Oh no,” says Frank. “Candy is not healthy. I will take a spinach donut.”

“Frank,” he says. “I do not think you get donuts.”

“Too bad,” says Frank. “I’m hungry.”

“Want to come with me?” Bean asks. “I’m nervous.”

“Why?” asks Frank.

Bean shakes in fear.

DONUTS
F

"Because Mad Dog might be there," he says.

"Who is Mad Dog?" asks Frank.

"Mad Dog is mean and scary," Bean says. "Mad Dog's food always wins. Nobody ever beats Mad Dog."

Frank has an idea.

"I will meet you there," he says.

DONUTS
FOXY TACOS
PIZZA
PANCAKES
ICE CREAM

Chapter 2

FOOD TRUCK FRIDAY

Bean rolls up.

He sees lots of other food trucks.

Fox sells tacos.

Crayon sells pizza.

Bear sells ice cream.

Mr. Pinecone sells pancakes.

Owl sells coffee.

Sloth sells slow-cooked soup.

"Phew!" says Bean. "Mad Dog is not here. Now I have a chance to win."

Bean plays his radio.

He puts up a wind man.

"HELLO! THE WAIT IS OVER!" he shouts. "IT IS I, BEAN!"

Frog reads Bean's menu.

"Care for a donut?" Bean asks.

"I do-*not*," says Frog. He hops away.

"I hope no other trucks come," Bean says.

But then he hears . . .

TOOT TOOT TOOT!

"Oh no," says Bean. "Is that Mad Dog?"

F
OATMEAL

“Frank!” Bean cries.

“Hello, Bean!” says Frank. “Care for some healthy oatmeal?”

DONUTS
DONUTS
OATMEAL
MENU
OATMEAL
(PLAIN)
F
ZEN OF STIR

Chapter 3

ZIP AND ZING

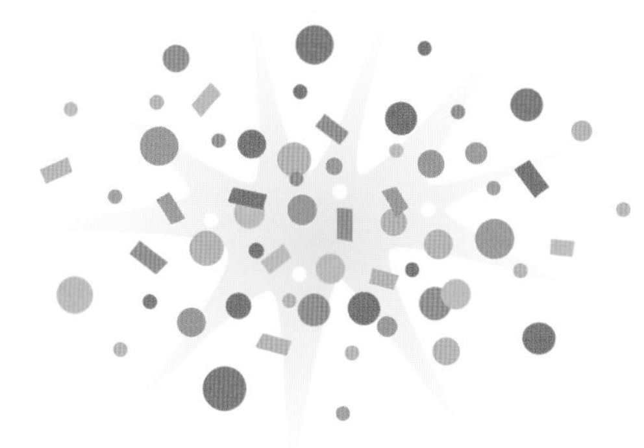

"Frank! What are you doing?" Bean asks.

"Surprise!" says Frank. "I am here. Now you won't feel nervous."

"You are a good friend," says Bean. "But now we are both trying to win the prize."

"Yes, isn't that fun?" asks Frank. "I wonder if I could win."

“With *oatmeal*?” says Bean.

“Everyone loves plain oatmeal,” says Frank.

“No,” says Bean. “Plain oatmeal is a bowl of sadness.”

“Oatmeal is good for you,” says Frank.

"It is missing zip!" says Bean. "It is missing zing! Food should make you want to sing."

"How can food make you want to sing?" Frank asks.

"Easy," said Bean. "The secret to good food is lots of toppings. Like these."

Bean adds sprinkles. "Zip!" he says.

He adds jam. “Zing!” he says.
He adds lots of this. “ZIP!”
He adds lots of that. “ZING!”
ZIP! ZING!

“There,” says Bean. “Try it.”
Frank takes a bite.
He chews. He thinks.
“I do not hear singing,” says Bean.

“Too much zip,” says Frank. “Too much zing.”

“No such thing,” says Bean. “My donuts will win the prize.”

“My oatmeal might win,” says Frank.

But then they hear . . .

DING-A-LING-A-LING!

A new food truck is on the way.

Bean shakes in fear.

"Uh-oh," Crayon says. "Here comes Mad Dog!"

MAD DOG
CUPCAKES
1ST
1
MD

Chapter 4

THE OATMEAL SONG

This is Mad Dog.

These are Mad Dog's cupcakes.

These are Mad Dog's helpers.

These are Mad Dog's seventeen first-place ribbons.

Everything here is Mad Dog's.

MAD DOG
CUPCAKES
1ST
NO RETURNS
NO REFUNDS
NO CATS

Mad Dog smiles.

She blows kisses to her fans.

A long line forms.

“She does not look mad to me,” says Frank.

Mad Dog barks at a kitten.

“No cats allowed!” she yells.

Mad Dog roars at her helpers.

"Move faster!" she orders.

"Oh my!" says Frank. "She *is* a mad dog. Look at how fast she makes her helpers work."

“Aha!” says Bean. “Working fast must be the secret to good food.”

“They are working too fast,” says Frank. “Look at their ears!”

Frank sits.

Bean speeds. “More zip!” he says.

Frank hums.

Bean hurries. “More zing!” he says.

But nobody lines up for their trucks.

Frank stands.

Bean sobs.

"I haven't sold one donut," he cries.

Just then, someone lines up for Bean's truck.

"I would like a donut, please," says Frank. "May I pay with oatmeal?"

“Yes!” Bean cheers.

Oops! Donut toppings fly everywhere!

“Oh no,” says Bean. “Look what I did to my donuts.”

“Look what you did to my oatmeal,” Frank says.

Frank tries it.

"Yum!" he says.

Bean tries it.

"This oatmeal is a bowl of happy," he says.

Together they make up a song.

"With just enough zip
and just enough zing,
this oatmeal makes us want to sing!"

Frank and Bean have an idea. . . .

ZIP
ZING
FRIENDSHIP BOWLS
DONUTS

Everyone loves Frank and Bean's Friendship Bowls.

(Well, almost everyone.)

Together, they sing the Oatmeal Song.

"Oatmeal, oatmeal, oh, oh, oh!
Oatmeal, oatmeal, now we know
what gives you zip,
what gives you zing.
You're made with joy.
That's why we sing!
Oh, oh, oh, oatmeal!"

"Now I know the secret to good food," says Bean.

"Me too," says Frank. "Food tastes best when you share it with a friend."

The end!